A MAGIC CIRCLE BOOK

A HORSE FOR MATTHEW ALLEN

by **VIRGINIA KESTER SMILEY**

photography by **BRYAN HOPKINS**

THEODORE CLYMER
SENIOR AUTHOR, READING 360

GINN AND COMPANY
A XEROX COMPANY

Home Office, Lexington, Massachusetts 02173

Library of Congress Catalog Card Number: 70–153911

International Standard Book Number: 0-663-22980-4

Matthew Allen stood beside the ticket window and stared thoughtfully at the shiny black horse he called Jet. Somehow, riding his favorite horse helped him forget how much he hated the hot, crowded city. He missed the farm where he had grown up, and he missed the farm horse he loved.

Matthew remembered how one night Uncle Jim had phoned and said there was a job waiting for Pa if he wanted it. The bus company where Uncle Jim worked needed drivers. He said that Pa could make more money, and there was room to live in the same house with Aunt Delia and him.

Matthew sighed. The house was O.K., and it was fun being with Uncle Jim and Aunt Delia. But still he missed the farm.

Mr. Wilson, the merry-go-round man, stepped behind the ticket window. "All right, cowboy, let's go. I'll be starting the ride in a few minutes."

Matthew dug into the pocket of his jeans and took out fifty cents. "I'll take ten tickets," he said.

TICKET
Park
38068

Mr. Wilson slid the tickets out the window. Matthew tore one ticket off and put the rest in his pocket. Then as he walked toward Jet, he saw Roger Marsh running through the gate. Knowing that Roger would try to get to Jet first, Matthew began running too. He reached the merry-go-round and swung up beside Jet, just two steps ahead of Roger.

"I'm taking this horse!" Roger cried, pushing Matthew away.

Matthew shook his head. "Oh, no, you're not, Roger. He's mine."

Roger made a fist and held it in front of Matthew's face. "Want to make something out of it?" he said in a low voice. Then he saw Mr. Wilson coming toward them and turned away. "I don't care," he said. "Go ahead and ride that horse. I'll get him next time. You just wait and see." Roger walked over to another horse and got on.

Matthew climbed onto Jet and whispered, "It's me, Jet."

The merry-go-round started turning, slowly at first and then faster and faster. Matthew closed his eyes and imagined that he was riding Al, the farm horse. For a few minutes it seemed as if he was back home.

When the merry-go-round slowed down and finally stopped, Matthew tore off another ticket and waited for the next ride to begin. Suddenly Roger came alongside and grabbed his shirt. "C'mon," he said. "You've had your turn on that horse. It's my turn."

Matthew frowned. Why couldn't Roger ride the other horses and leave Jet for him? "Find another horse, Roger," he said firmly.

Roger was ready to pull Matthew off Jet, but the merry-go-round started turning again. "I'll come real early tomorrow," he warned. "Then *you* can find another horse!"

Matthew wasn't worried. Tomorrow was a long way off. He stayed on Jet for a few more rides. Then he remembered that he had promised to come home early.

When the merry-go-round stopped again, he slid off Jet's back and jumped off the platform. When he turned around and saw that Roger had mounted Jet, Matthew was angry. If only he hadn't said he would come home early, he'd still be on Jet. But if he went home now; his mother would let him come back to the park tomorrow. He pulled the tickets out of his pocket. There were still four left.

Mr. Wilson walked over. "There isn't much time left to ride, son. We'll be taking the merry-go-round down in a day or two. The city is going to build a skating rink here."

The news was like a bolt of lightning. Matthew had never dreamed that Jet might someday be gone. He turned again to glance at the horse, and Roger made a face. Sadly, Matthew started home.

The next day when Matthew sat down to breakfast, his mother looked at him with a worried frown. "Matthew, do you feel all right?" she asked. She put a bowl of cereal in front of him and felt his forehead. "You feel warm, son."

Matthew poked at the cereal with his spoon. "I'm O.K., Mama. I'm just not hungry." He couldn't let his mother know he didn't feel well. He still had tickets to use and he wanted to get to the park before Roger. "Please can I go to the park?" he begged.

From the look on her face he knew that the answer was No. "I'm sure the merry-go-round will be there tomorrow," she told him. "Try to eat your breakfast."

Matthew couldn't eat. He pushed the bowl away. His mother had said "tomorrow." Jet might be gone by then.

It was three days later when Matthew felt better and his mother told him he could go to the park. As soon as he finished breakfast, he stuffed the tickets into his pocket and headed for the park.

The day was beginning to get hot, but he didn't notice. He ran down the sidewalk, darting in and out among boys and girls on roller skates and bikes. At the corner he ran into Roger.

Roger grabbed Matthew's sleeve. "Hey! Why don't you watch where you're going! Say, where're you going anyway?"

Breathlessly, Matthew pointed at the park gate. Roger looked surprised. "Are you kidding? The merry-go-round is gone."

Matthew couldn't hear any music, but he didn't want to believe that Jet was gone. "Maybe Roger is teasing," he thought. Aloud he said, "It can't be gone. I still have tickets." And without waiting for an answer, he ran on toward the park.

When he got just inside the gate, he stopped running and looked around. Only the floor and roof of the merry-go-round remained. The men were packing the horses into a van.

Mr. Wilson waved to Matthew. "No more rides, son. The builders want to get started with the skating rink. They're moving in at noon."

For a while Matthew stood nearby watching sadly as Mr. Wilson and the men worked. Now and then they threw parts of the merry-go-round onto a pile.

"I'll be starting a bonfire soon to get rid of this trash," Mr. Wilson said. "Stay around and watch if you'd like."

Matthew shrugged his shoulders and walked slowly around the pile. He saw part of a saddle, a broken seat, a worn leather strap, and the oldest horse on the merry-go-round. Mr. Wilson had said he was going to throw it out. It was badly scratched and chipped. Matthew stood looking at the horse and thinking for a few moments and then turned to Mr. Wilson. "Can I have that old horse in the trash pile, Mr. Wilson?" he asked.

"Sure, cowboy. But you'll have to get it out of here by noon today. If you can't, I'll just have to burn it with the rest of the trash."

"I'm sure I can get him out," Matthew answered.

Mr. Wilson nodded and went back to work.

Matthew grabbed hold of the horse's head and pulled, but it was very heavy and wouldn't move. He tugged again with all his might and this time the horse moved a little. He groaned and wiped his forehead. With this much trouble, he could never get the horse home. He needed help.

It seemed to take forever until Matthew finally burst into the kitchen. His mother was washing clothes.

"You're in a big hurry," she said.

Without stopping to catch his breath, Matthew told his mother about the merry-go-round horse. "Mama, can you help me get him?" he begged. "He'll be burned with the trash if we don't hurry. Please, Mama? Right now?"

His mother shook her head and said, "Matthew, you don't need that old horse."

"Can't I have him? I'll keep him out in the garage," he pleaded.

She thought for a moment and said, "Oh, well, I guess you can have it. But I can't help you. I've got to get these clothes done and be at work by noon. Maybe your father will help you when he comes home."

"But Pa won't be home until suppertime. That'll be too late," he whined.

"I'm sorry, Matthew," she said. "Aunt Delia's not here and I can't help you."

It was no use. He couldn't have the horse. Matthew sat down and stared out the window while his mother finished the wash. Suddenly he jumped up shouting "The buggy!" and ran out to the garage.

Against the wall was the old baby buggy he had found the day they moved in. As he pulled it out, one corner fell down with a bang. "Oh, no!" he cried. "I can't carry the horse in this busted thing."

Feeling very unhappy, he walked around to the front steps and sat down. He could see the dark smoke rising over the park. "I wish I could have had that old horse," he thought. "If only I had a way to get him home."

He watched the smoke rise for a few more minutes. Then as he stood up to go inside, he glanced down the street and saw Roger pulling his wagon. Forgetting that the horse might already be in the bonfire, Matthew ran down the block shouting, "Can I use your wagon, Roger?"

He could see that Roger was about to say No, and he really couldn't blame Roger. All summer he had been selfish with Jet, and Jet really belonged to everyone. Roger had a good reason to say No.

"I've got a chance to get an old horse from Mr. Wilson," Matthew said excitedly. "If you help me, he can be half yours."

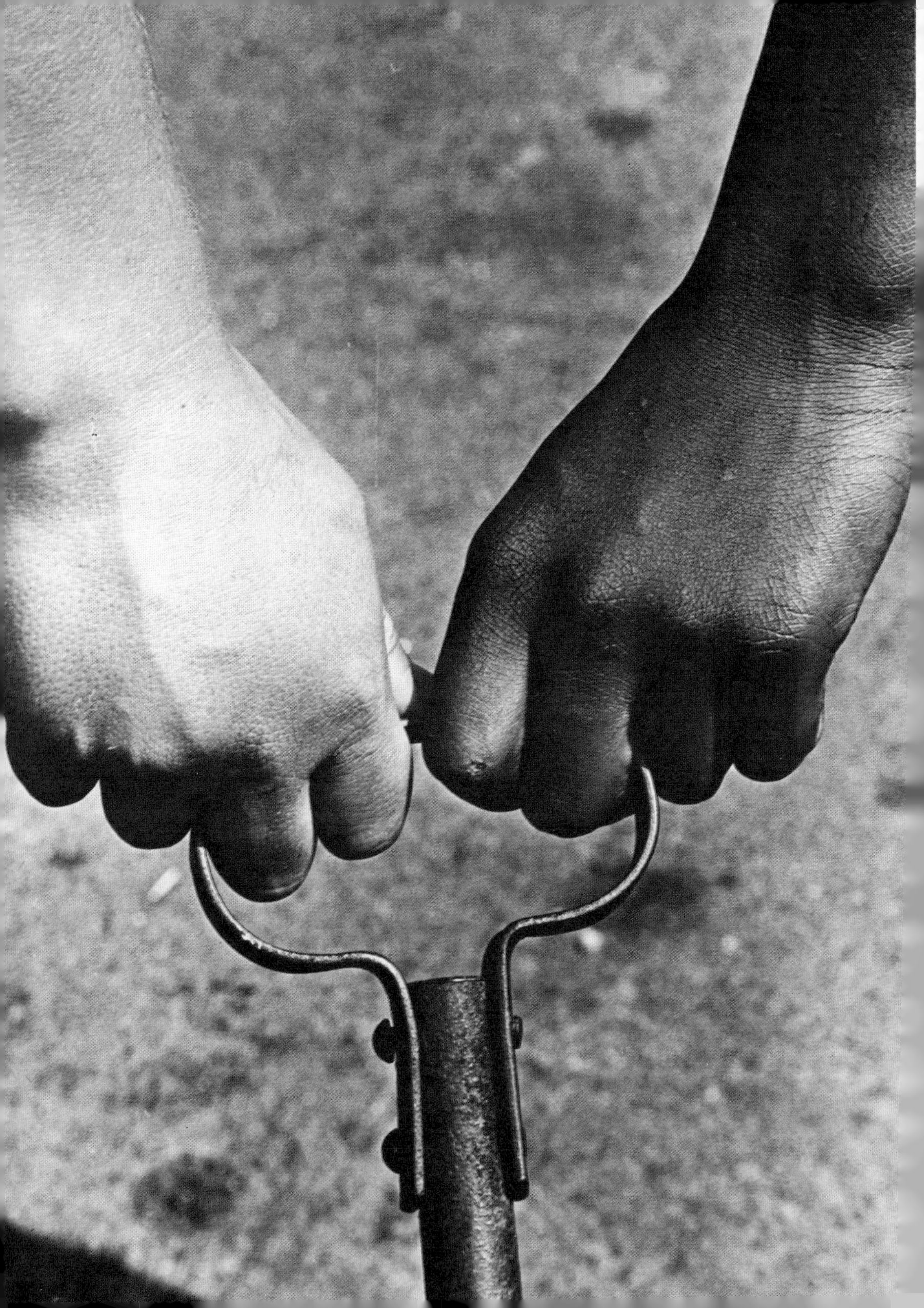

"You're saying that just so you can use my wagon," Roger said, frowning.

Matthew shook his head. "No, I'm not, Roger. I promise to share him."

Roger didn't answer at first. Then he yanked Matthew's arm and said, "O.K. But remember, if we use my wagon, the horse is half mine." And without wasting another minute, both boys grabbed the wagon handle and raced toward the park. They stopped outside the gate and looked at the van all packed and ready to go. Mr. Wilson saw the boys and waved them in.

"I was hoping you'd get here in time, cowboy. I couldn't burn this old horse — not when I knew he could have a boy like you to look after him."

"Gee, thanks, Mr. Wilson," Matthew said, smiling. "I was sure hoping he wasn't burned up yet."

Mr. Wilson helped them put the horse on the wagon, and the boys started home. When they paused for a rest, Matthew asked, "What should we call our horse?"

Roger thought a moment and answered, "I don't know. Let's wait until we fix him up to name him. O.K.?"

Matthew ran his hand over the chipped wood. "I'd like to call him Jet," he thought. But aloud he said, "O.K." and he whistled all the way home.

ABCDEFGHIJ 7654321
PRINTED IN THE UNITED STATES OF AMERICA